W9-BSL-927

AND THERE WAS

EVENING

ערב

בוקר

AND THERE WAS

MORNING

KAR-BEN PUBLISHING, INC.
A division of Lerner Publishing Group, Inc.
241 First Avenue North
Minneapolis, MN 55401 USA
1-800-4-KARBEN

Website address: www.karben.com

Main body text set in Baskerville MT Std 17/20.
Typeface provided by Monotype Typography.

Library of Congress Cataloging-in-Publication Data

Names: Zager, Ellen Kahan, author, illustrator. | Helfand, Harriet, author.
Title: And there was evening and there was morning / by Ellen Kahan Zager and Harriet Cohen Helfand ; illustrated by Ellen Kahan Zager.
Description: Minneapolis : Kar-Ben Publishing, [2018] | Series: Bible | Summary: Illustrations and simple, rhyming text present the seven days of creation.
Identifiers: LCCN 2017030340| ISBN 9781512483642 (lb) | ISBN 9781512483659 (pb) | ISBN 9781541524026 (eb pdf)
Subjects: | CYAC: Stories in rhyme. | Creation—Fiction.
Classification: LCC PZ8.3.Z24 And 2018 | DDC [E]—dc23

LC record available at https://lccn.loc.gov/2017030340

Manufactured in the United States of America
1-43362-33174-12/13/2017

AND THERE WAS EVENING
AND THERE WAS MORNING

Harriet Cohen Helfand and Ellen Kahan Zager
Illustrated by Ellen Kahan Zager

Day One

The world began when God said "light,"
And changed the world from dark to bright.
Dark in the night and light in the day,
Our beautiful world was underway.

And there was evening and there was morning, a single day.

Day Two

For water above and water below,
God spoke the words so waters would flow.
Down to the sea, waves rushing by,
And up to the clouds, high in the sky.

And there was evening and there was morning, a watery day.

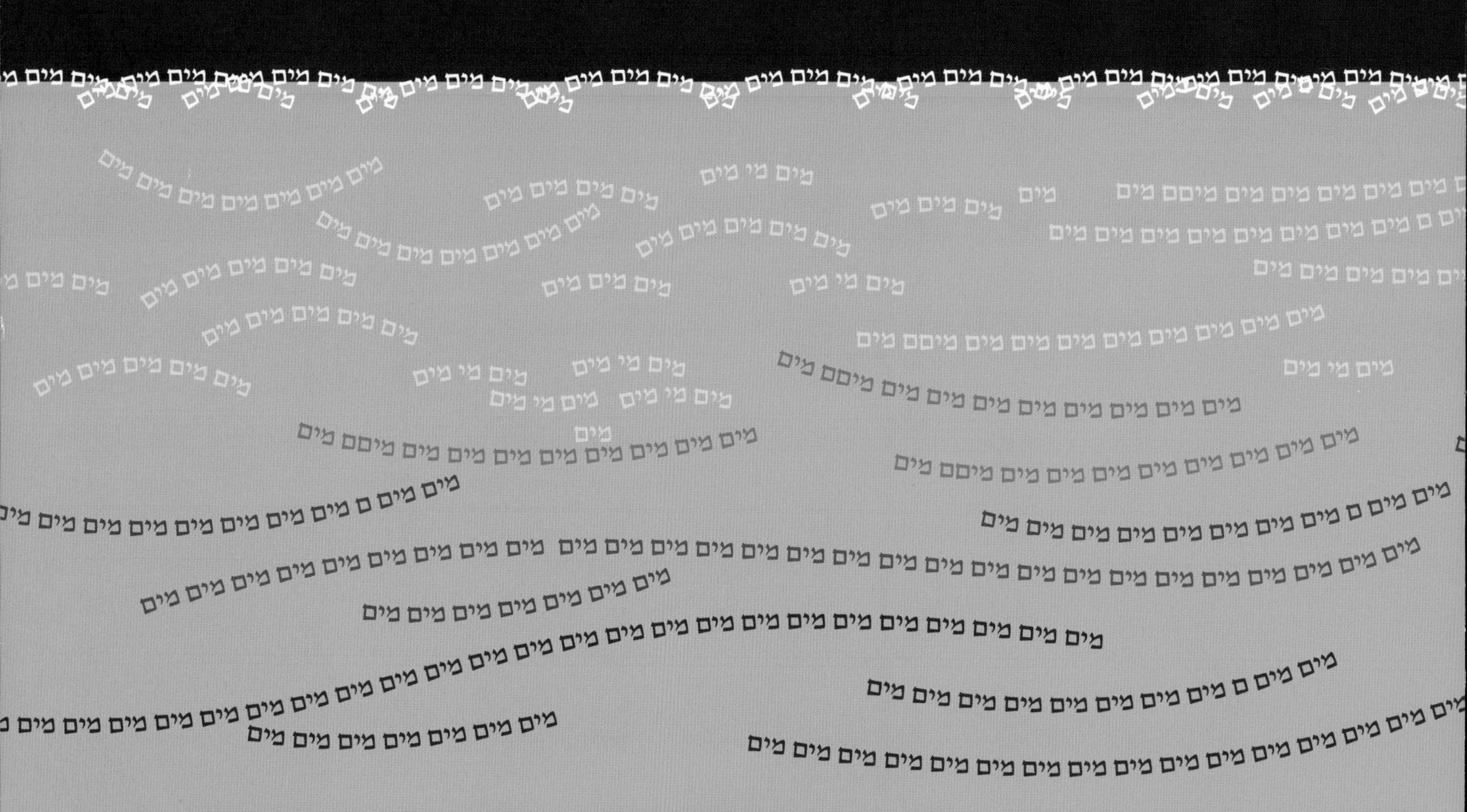

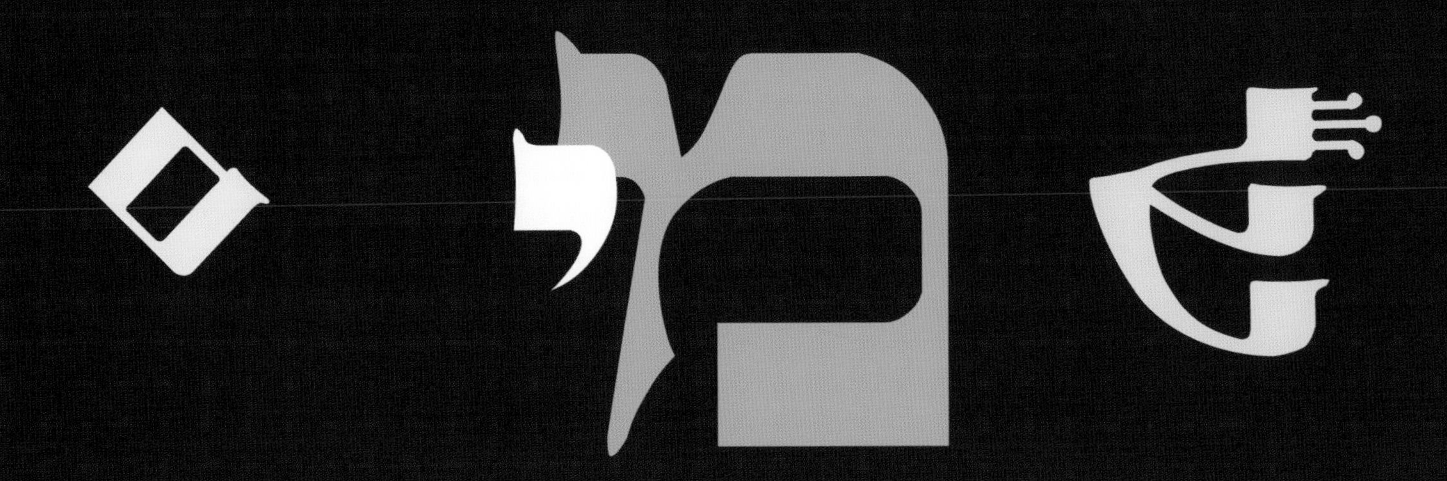
מים

Day Three

God separated land from sea,
And by more words there came to be,
Fruits ripe and round, blooms and seeds,
Sprigs and herbs and vines and trees.

And there was evening and there was morning, a fruitful day.

Day Four

The sun, the moon, and stars that shine,
High above to mark off time,
God set in place so we'd find our way,
Evening to evening, and day to day.

And there was evening and there was morning, a peaceful day.

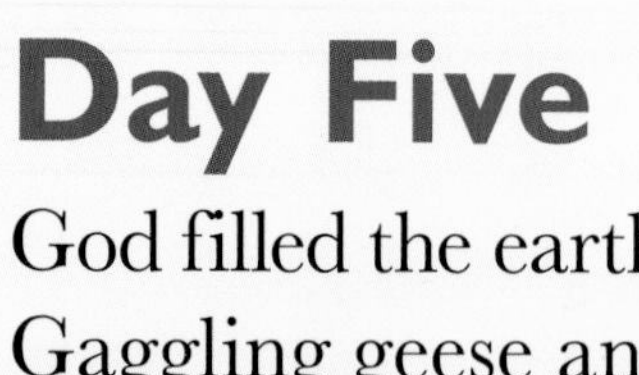

Day Five

God filled the earth with pikes and jays,
Gaggling geese and manta rays,
Birds that soar across the sky,
Fishes swimming, gliding by.

And there was evening and there was morning,
a noisy day.

סוס
סוס
סוס

Day Six

More and more living things God brought forth,
East and west and south and north.
Creatures that slither and crawl and alight,
Beasts that run wild and howl in the night.

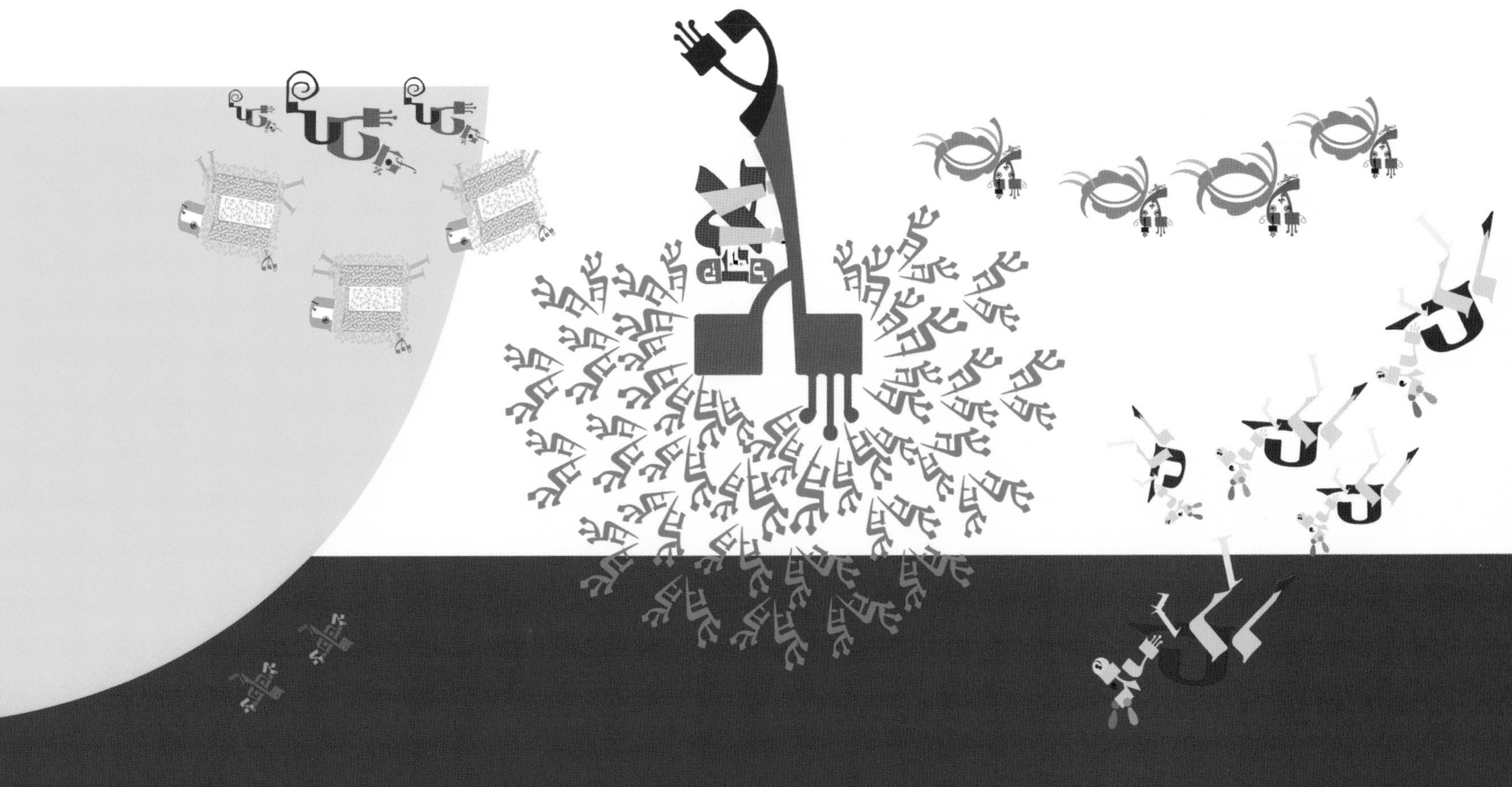

For taking good care of this marvelous plan,
God spoke the words that made woman and man.
To watch over all beings who live in the sky,
The sea and the land, and all you can spy.

And now as this glorious masterpiece stood,
God looked at the world and declared "very good."

And there was evening and there was morning,
A lively day.

The heavens and the earth, and all they contain, were completed.

On the seventh day God completed the work which God had been doing;
God ceased on the seventh day
from all the work which God had done.
Then God blessed the seventh day and called it holy,
because on it God ceased from all God's work of Creation.

Shabbat

After six days of work, God took a rest,
And named Shabbat, a day to be blessed.
A holy day, and now we rest too,
So we can begin each week anew.

And there is evening and there is morning . . .

English	Transliteration/Hebrew	
sun	shemesh	שֶׁמֶשׁ
evening/ morning	erev/ boker	עֶרֶב/ בֹּקֶר
sky	shamayim	שָׁמַיִם
water	mayim	מַיִם
pomegranate	rimon	רִמוֹן
date	tamar	תָּמָר
figs	t'aynim	תְּאֵנִים
vine	gefen	גֶּפֶן
barley	s'orah	שְׂעוֹרָה
wheat	chitah	חִטָּה
olives	zaytim	זֵיתִים
star	cochav	כּוֹכָב

English	Transliteration/Hebrew	
bird	tzipor	צִפּוֹר
tuna	tuna	טוּנָה
turkey	tarnegol hodu	תַּרְנְגוֹל-הוֹדוּ
manta ray	manta ray	מַנְטָה רֵיי
owl	yanshuf	יַנְשׁוּף
tree	etz	עֵץ
goose	avaz	אַוָּז
jay	orvani	עוֹרְבָנִי
bird	tzipor	צִפּוֹר
pike	kidon	כִּידוֹן
squid	dionun	דְּיוֹנוּן
giraffe	ghirafa	גִ'רָפָה
horse	soos	סוּס

English	Transliteration/Hebrew	
leopard/ tiger	*namer/ tigris*	נָמֵר/טִיגְרִיס
deer	*tzvi*	צְבִי
bear	*dov*	דֹּב
snake	*nachash*	נָחָשׁ
camel	*gamal*	גָּמָל
lion	*aryeh*	אַרְיֵה
pine	*oren*	אֹרֶן
penguin	*pingvin*	פִּנְגְּוִין
walrus	*soos-yam*	סוּס יָם
polar bear	*dov kotev*	דֹּב קוֹטֶב
lizard	*l'ta-ah*	לְטָאָה
sheep	*keves*	כֶּבֶשׂ
goat	*ez*	עֵז

English	Transliteration/Hebrew	
flower	*perach*	פֶּרַח
koala	*koala*	קוֹאָלָה
kangaroo	*kanguru*	קֶנְגּוּרוּ
man	*adam*	אָדָם
rose	*shoshana*	שׁוֹשַׁנָּה
leaf	*aleh*	עָלֶה
cypress	*brosh*	בְּרוֹשׁ
garlic	*shum*	שׁוּם
turtle	*tzav*	צָב
hippopatamus	*hipopotam*	הִיפּוֹפּוֹטָם
peacock	*tavas*	טַוָּס
spider	*akavish*	עַכָּבִישׁ
whale	*livyatan*	לִוְיָתָן

Artist's Note

We understand that God created the world with words. The pictures in this book are also created with words. Because Hebrew is the language of the Torah, these images are in Hebrew. Each image is created with the Hebrew letters for that word. In cases where I needed more letters than are in the word to finish the image, I used dingbats, numbers, English letters or abstract shapes.
–E.K.Z.

About the Author and Artist

Harriet Cohen Helfand has enjoyed writing since she was a child. As a lover of the Hebrew language, she wanted to create a poem that reflects the words of creation in the Torah. **Ellen Kahan Zager** has served the Jewish community in many ways with her creative abilities, from designing museum installations to serving on Jewish organization and day school boards. Harriet and Ellen live in Baltimore.